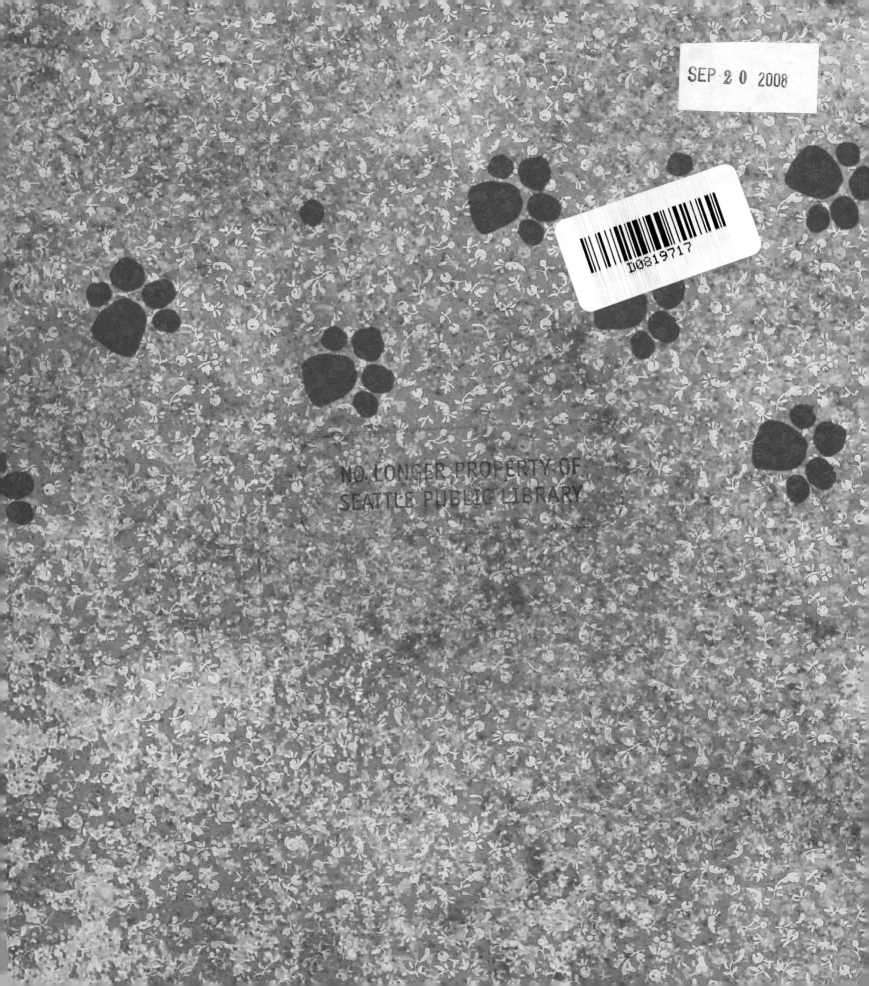

For Donald

Kane/Miller Book Publishers, Inc.
First American Edition 2008
by Kane/Miller Book Publishers, Inc.
La Jolla, California

Originally published in Australia by Random House Australia Pty Ltd, 2008

Copyright © Colin Thompson 2008

All rights reserved. For information contact:
Kane/Miller Book Publishers, Inc.
P.O. Box 8515
La Jolla, CA 92038
www.kanemiller.com

Library of Congress Control Number: 2008920674
Printed and bound in China
1 2 3 4 5 6 7 8 9 10

ISBN: 978-1-933605-90-6

The BIG LITTLE BOOK of HAPPY SADNESS

Colin Thompson

Kane/Miller
BOOK PUBLISHERS

George lived alone with his grandmother and an empty
place where his mother and father should have been.

George's grandmother was a kind lady, but she was very old and the two of them spent most of their lives on different planets.

Most Friday afternoons on his way home from school, in that time before the weekend when lonely people realize just how lonely they are, George visited the dog shelter. And he always seemed to end up by the last cage in the last aisle. Even the concrete had given up down there. Hidden in the shade of a huge tree, where the sun never bothered to go, the concrete and the cages sat beneath a coat of verdigris.

The last cage was where the dogs no one wanted went for a final week before their journey to heaven. George felt at home there. In the dark gloom, he found a place where everything seemed lonelier than he was.

The last cage was often empty, and any dog that did find itself in there usually hid in the shadows, unseen and unloved . . . until one special Friday, George arrived and found a dog sitting at the front of the cage looking at him.

George stared at the dog and the dog stared at George and they both knew they were seeing a reflection of themselves.

The dog, like George, was scruffy and sad. Yet
even at the end of the line, he was quietly dignified
and seemed to accept his fate.

Here was a dog George could really identify with.

"The last dog," said George to the lady in the office.

"Last dog?"

"Yes, the one down the end," said George.

"Oh, yes, poor thing, it's his final day today," she said.

"Can I take him?"

"We are talking about the same dog, aren't we?" she asked. "The three-legged one in the last cage."

George nodded.

"Why would you want him? We've got eighty-seven other dogs here. They've all got four legs and bright eyes and a coat that doesn't look like it's covered in lard," said the woman. "Why not take one of them?"

"No. I want the last dog," said George.

"He's called Jeremy," said the woman, "and you'll have to ask your parents first. We close in one hour."

George ran home faster than he had ever run before - so fast that all the air and words were sucked out of him.

"Dog, dog, Jeremy!" was all he could manage.

"Slow down, slow down," said George's grandmother.

"No time. Dog!" said George.

"We'll have to think about this," said the old lady. "It's a big decision. You know what they say: 'A dog isn't just for Christmas, it's for life.'"

"But he won't have a life tomorrow," said George and finally managed to tell her about Jeremy.

His grandmother saw the big empty place inside George and got her coat. "You go on ahead," she said. "I'll catch up."

George ran back and caught the office lady, who was getting ready to leave. They waited for George's grandmother together.

In his cage, Jeremy waited too. Curled up in his basket he watched the sky grow dark and closed his eyes.

And then his cage opened for the last time.

"But it's not morning yet," thought Jeremy. "I didn't even get my last dream."

There was the little round boy who had looked at him before, and an old lady. They were both smiling at him. And they didn't take him towards the green door that led to the big kennel in the sky; they turned left and went back to the office.

The dog shelter lady gave Jeremy a bright blue collar and leash and a disc with his name on it. They were the first ones he had ever owned because no one had wanted to take him for a walk before. People don't when you've only got three legs. A walk isn't so much a walk as a hobble followed by a falling over, a getting up and then doing it all over again.

After it had taken five minutes just to reach the shelter's gate, George picked Jeremy up and carried him home.

Jeremy had never been indoors before. When George lifted him onto an armchair in front of the fire, Jeremy thought that maybe he had gone through the green door after all and died and gone to heaven.

In the next few weeks Jeremy learned a whole new vocabulary, full of words like "cushion" and "dinner" and "cuddle." George's world was filled with words he had heard but never experienced before, like "warmth" and "not being on your own."

The one word they both wanted to add was "walkies." But they needed one more leg for that. So George and his grandmother decided to do something about it: they would make Jeremy a leg.

Neither of them were very good at making things, so they started modestly. They mixed up flour-and-water paste and built a leg out of newspaper. They included the new TV guide even though it was only Tuesday, which just goes to show how much they loved Jeremy.

It's one of the great faults of nature that dogs can't smile, because when Jeremy ran around the garden on his new leg, he had a grin inside his head as wide as Australia. He ran over to the tree and, for the first time in his life, lifted his leg. Of course, only having three legs he could have done the same thing without having to lift one, but he always got muddled up, lifted the wrong leg and ended up flat on his face with a wet tummy. Not any more!

But then his new leg got wet and collapsed. So George's grandmother baked Jeremy a pastry leg. But Jeremy kept eating it.

Finally, George sharpened his penknife and carved Jeremy a wooden leg like pirates wear. Then he made a second leg with a wheel on the bottom so they could play soccer in the park, and a third leg with a slipper on the end for bedtime.

The empty place inside George didn't seem so empty any more.
And the three of them lived happily ever after for a very long time.

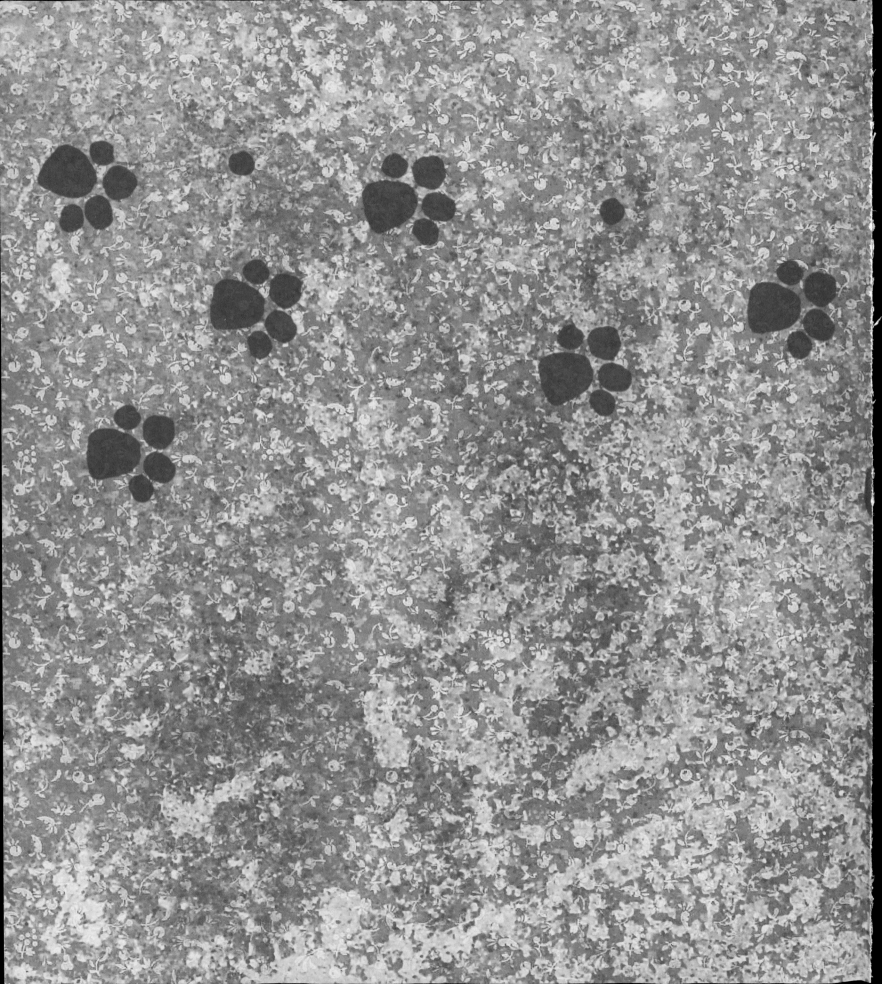